My Horrible Secret

OTHER YEARLING BOOKS YOU WILL ENJOY:

YEARLING BOOKS/YOUNG YEARLINGS/YEARLING CLASSICS are designed especially to entertain and enlighten young people. Charles F. Reasoner, Professor Emeritus of Children's Literature and Reading, New York University, is consultant to this series.

For a complete listing of all Yearling titles,
write to Dell Readers Service, P.O. Box 1045,
South Holland, Illinois 60473.

My Horrible Secret

by Stephen Roos

ILLUSTRATED BY CAROL NEWSOM

A Yearling Book

Published by
Dell Publishing Co., Inc.
1 Dag Hammarskjold Plaza
New York, New York 10017

Yearling ® TM 913705, Dell Publishing Co., Inc.

ISBN: 0-440-43956-6

Printed in the United States of America

A hardcover edition of this work is available
from Delacorte Press, 1 Dag Hammarskjold Plaza
New York, New York

May 1983

10 9 8 7

CW

For my mother and father

Contents

CHAPTER ONE

My Horrible Secret

You're probably wondering why I decided to let you in on my horrible secret. Here I am living in mortal fear that someone is going to uncover the truth and I go shooting off my mouth to a complete and total stranger. I wouldn't blame you for thinking that my horrible secret is that I'm the dumbest eleven-year-old kid in the world.

If that's what you think, you're dead wrong. The truth is that I'm just about the smartest kid in Miss Presley's fifth grade. So far this year I've even tied with mean old Claire Van Kemp. The thing is that secrets are a lot of fun to hear, but they're not much fun to keep, especially if they're yours. I guess that's why they say that confession is good for the soul. They usually don't bother to add that it's even better if you spill the beans to someone who won't go and blab it all over town. That's how you got the once-in-a-lifetime chance to hear the truth, the whole truth, and nothing but the truth from yours truly.

Now you're probably wondering why I'm so sure I can trust you. How do I know that you've never been to New Eden? How can I be so sure that you're not living here right now? Well, if you weren't impressed with me before, what you hear next should really knock your socks off.

You see, there is no such place as New Eden. At least, none that I've ever heard of. And just for the record, I'd better tell you that my name is not Warren Fingler. I made that up and it's not anything like my real name. The part about me being eleven years old is true. It's also true that I'm just a little under five feet tall and I weigh a little over ninety pounds. I'm sorry, but that's all the personal description you're going to get from me. And just to make extra sure that I can trust you, I've changed the names of all the other people, too. It's not to protect them, mind you. It's to protect me. Just the thought of someone in New Eden finding out sends chills up and down my spine.

A couple of times I thought of asking Mom and Dad if we could move to another town, but I have a pretty strong feeling they wouldn't go for the idea. Dad has lived in New Eden all his life and nothing about the place seems to bother him.

Mom is the only member of the family who hasn't spent all her life in New Eden. She moved here when she married Dad. Two years ago she opened up a bookstore that she calls The Book Worm and everyone else calls The Worm. I don't think there's anything that could get her to leave, even if she didn't have the store.

Which brings me to Roger. Roger is my older brother and he's a sophomore at New Eden High and already he has won a letter for every sport he plays. Even now, everyone in town is saying that in two years he's going to be the first person in the history of the school to be captain of the football team, the hockey team, and the baseball team. If Roger could have his wish, he'd stay at New Eden High forever. Considering his grades, he just might.

Roger takes being a jock very seriously. When he gets up in the morning, the first thing he does is spend thirty minutes doing push-ups, sit-ups, and deep knee bends. After that, he puts on his sweat pants and sweat shirt and his running shoes and runs three miles. When he gets home, he throws a lot of raw vegetables and raw milk (which is as horrible as it sounds) and a protein supplement into the blender. It's a very noisy

3

blender and it's the first sound I hear in the morning. Ever since Roger entered the world of superstar jockdom, I haven't had to set my alarm clock.

This morning, like every other morning, Roger yelled, "Okay, Chump," as he jogged up the stairs on his way to take a shower. "It's time to rise and shine!"

"I don't want to rise," I said, pulling the blankets over my head. "And I don't want to shine, either. And stop calling me 'Chump.'"

Usually Roger just ignores me and jogs along to the bathroom, but today he walked into my room and pulled the covers away.

"Look, Chump," he said impatiently, "when they ship you off to Camp Hit-a-Homer this summer, you're going to be getting up at six thirty in the morning whether you like it or not."

Now I was awake. And I was mad, too. With only a few words Roger had ruined my entire day.

"I am not going to Camp Hit-a-Homer," I said. "Not ever."

"That's not what *they* say," Roger said. "They" is what Roger and I call Mom and Dad.

"I don't have to go if I don't want to. Mom and Dad aren't going to make me go."

"You know something, Warren?" Roger said. "You're turning into a real creep."

4

"It must be something I caught from you," I said.

"Say what you like, Warren. There's nothing like Camp Hit-a-Homer for turning kids into sports stars. And I'm the one who ought to know. If I hadn't gone there when *I* was eleven, I might not be the superstar athlete you see before you right now."

"Not everyone wants to be a jock," I said. "Some of us have higher goals in life."

Roger smiled the superior way he always does when he's talking about sports. "Don't kid me," he said. "There's nothing like being a superstar sports hero and you know it."

"If Camp Hit-a-Homer is going to make me just like you," I said, "I definitely don't want to go."

"Look, Warren," he said. "I'm only trying to help. If you want to stay a creep, that's your business."

"Get lost, Roger."

"Sure, sure," he said, beginning to back off. "But don't blame me when they give you the Creep of the Year award. Okay, Chump?"

Roger walked out of the room. In a minute I could hear the water running in the shower. By the time he had turned it off and jogged back downstairs, I was almost ready to face another day.

I went downstairs for the kind of breakfast regular humans eat. By that time Roger was drinking the last of his health food glop and finishing the sports page. Actually, Roger doesn't read the sports page so much as he memorizes it. Batting averages and intercepted passes are Roger's two main areas of conversation. If he knows who the President of the United States is, he's keeping it to himself.

As I poured myself some orange juice and smothered my cornflakes with sugar, it was Roger's cue to remind me of what I was doing to my organs. I pretended not to listen to him. I like cornflakes and sugar and I like them every single morning. Besides, seven thirty is too early to contemplate making any changes in your lifestyle.

The real reason I always have the same breakfast is that everyone in our house has to make his own and clean up afterward. When Mom opened The Worm, she explained that she was retiring as our full-time maid and bottle washer for gainful employment elsewhere. No longer was she going to spend her life cleaning up after a husband and two sons who were capable of cleaning up after themselves. If you stick to the one-glass-

and-one-cereal-bowl breakfast, the cleaning-up part comes to rinsing a couple of things and putting them in the dishwasher.

Just rinsing out the blender is too much for Roger. The guy is a bundle of energy when it comes to being a jock, but he falls apart when it comes to everything else. Although he can jog ten miles a day, he looks like a frightened pup if we miss the school bus and have to walk to school. Or if he's watching TV on Sunday afternoon, he waits until someone comes into the den to switch the channel from the movie to *Wide World of Sports*. Stacking the dishwasher and putting out the garbage use the wrong kinds of muscles, he says.

As far as I'm concerned, Roger doesn't have to lift a finger when he's at home. Sometimes after dinner Dad says it might be a nice idea if Roger and I went outside and played catch. Whenever he says it, I can feel my heart skip a beat or two while I wait for Roger to say that he's too tired. Then Dad frowns a little and I try to hide my relief.

If there's one person in the world I don't want finding out my secret, it's Roger, the superjock.

CHAPTER TWO

The Next Stop to Heaven

The main reason I can't tell *anyone* else about my secret is that New Eden is a very small town. The last census said that practically nobody lives here. Living in a small town means everyone knows everything about everyone. It means no detail is too unimportant to become a major topic of conversation.

"Did you hear the dentist over in Ridgewood says Marcie Lewis is going to need braces next year?" someone might say over the dinner table.

"I'm not surprised," someone else will say. "The whole Lewis family should have been enrolled in some group dental plan years ago. That Lewis overbite, you know."

"Did you see George Fuller reading a copy of *Your Neurotic Teenager* in the line at the bank yesterday?" someone else asks.

"Can't say I'm surprised," someone says back. "Freddie Fuller is turning into a real sassy kid. If his old man doesn't do something now, Freddie's going to end up on the wrong side of the law."

Or how about someone saying, "Did you hear about Warren Fingler"?

To which the reply is, "You mean Roger Fingler's kid brother?"

"That's the one. You heard about him yet?"

"Who hasn't? Everyone's talking about it."

"Always thought there was something funny about that kid. Imagine a big athlete like Roger Fingler having a nerdy brother like that. It's a real shame."

As you can see, no one in New Eden is ever very surprised about the calamities that happen to their neighbors, but they sure do feel sorry. One thing's for sure. I'm not going to let them feel sorry for me if I can help it. And I'm not going to let anyone call me a nerd.

I'm calling this chapter "The Next Stop to Heaven" because that's what everyone here calls New Eden. That's because New Eden is the last stop on the railroad line and there's a big sign at the station that reads WELCOME TO NEW EDEN and below it are the words THE NEXT STOP TO HEAVEN. Right across the street, in the center of the village green, stands what's left of the statue of Matthew Bumkis sitting on a horse. About two hundred years ago, Matthew Bumkis got New Eden going and last winter a bolt of lightning blew off his head. Now everyone calls him "the Headless Horseman."

As far as everyone else is concerned, New Eden is heaven, not just the next stop to it. In fact, I'm one of the few people who would like to buy a one-way bus ticket out. The only other person I know who wants out is Arthur Lomax and everyone in town knows why he's leaving. His parents are even saving up money to help him.

Arthur started taking music lessons when he was five and now, at the ripe old age of eleven, he says he's going to be a concert pianist when he grows up. When he's eighteen he's going to go to a music conservatory instead of college. Most of the people in New Eden think that's kind of strange, but his parents, Mr. and Mrs. Lomax, are very proud of him, so everyone else here says they're proud of him, too.

I've known Arthur all my life and he's in Miss Presley's fifth grade, but he sits two rows behind me because he's an "L" and I'm an "F." I guess Arthur is my best friend, but we don't have an awful lot to say to one another. Arthur spends every afternoon practicing on the piano, so I spend most of my time talking to Mrs. Lomax. If she's busy, I turn on the television. Around four o'clock, Mrs. Lomax brings in some sandwiches and I turn off the set and Arthur stops playing. Then the three of us talk for a while and I go home.

Unlike some other parents I could name, Mrs. Lomax never suggests that we go out and play ball. She's really the best part about hanging out with Arthur.

It was the beginning of April when Mrs. Lomax caught me off guard.

"Do you think it's such a good idea to watch all those soap operas all afternoon?" she asked, very gently. "I'm not criticizing, you know. I was just wondering if there isn't something you'd rather do after school."

"I can't think of anything, Mrs. Lomax," I said, knowing that there was no way I could tell her that I was using her house as a hideout from the baseball games that went on every afternoon in New Eden from the middle of April until the end of August. "Well, maybe I have some homework I could do at home," I said.

"I just thought you might want to play with some of the other boys," she said. "I'm sure Arthur wouldn't mind. He's so tied up with his music."

Personally, I didn't think that Arthur would

notice if I was there or not, but I didn't say that to Mrs. Lomax. It would have made her feel bad.

"Good-bye, Mrs. Lomax," I said. "Thanks for the sandwich."

"Good-bye, Warren," she said. "Maybe you'll come by tomorrow, dear. You're always welcome."

Mrs. Lomax meant what she said about my always being welcome, but I had a feeling my number was up. That's why I decided to see if my only other friend in New Eden was at home.

Her name is Laurel O'Connor and I like her a lot, even though she is old enough to be my older sister. If you knew her you'd be surprised that we're friends and only partly because of the age difference.

Laurel is a freshman in high school, just a year behind Roger, and I got to know her because she had this really weird crush on Roger. The reason she got all soft on Roger is because he's the only human being in New Eden who is better at sports than she is. It can't be because of his personality.

I found out about Laurel last winter when she started telephoning Roger after dinner. I guess I don't have to mention that Roger gets a lot of calls from girls on account of his being a super-star. Not that he minds. For about two hours after dinner he keeps the wires humming with all of them, except for Laurel. He didn't like talking with her at all, maybe because she knows even more about sports than he does. I guess it made him feel inferior.

Every time the phone rang, Roger would yell at me, "If it's her, tell her I'm at the library." We all knew that "her" was Laurel and usually it was. I'd try to tell her as sincerely as I could that Roger was at the library, which would be pretty hard for anyone who knew Roger better than Laurel did to believe. I guess I was so convincing that Laurel didn't pick up on the message that Roger just didn't want to talk with her. But that's how Laurel and I started to become friends and that's how I found out that she didn't think New Eden was exactly the next stop to heaven either. When she finishes high school, Laurel wants to go to a college where they take women's athletics seriously. Until I met Laurel I didn't know that being a jock wasn't all roses. I guess it's different if you're a girl.

One day after school, when I was on my way over to Arthur's house, Laurel made this big point of coming up to me and asking if I would like to have a Coke with her. You can imagine how surprised I was. High school girls wouldn't be caught dead with an eleven-year-old boy.

14

"Order whatever you like," she said as soon as we'd sat down in a booth at the Hot Shoppe. "You don't have to have a Coke if you don't want to."

"In that case, I'll have the double banana split with fudge sauce," I said. Chances like this didn't come along every day.

"I wanted to ask you something," Laurel said once the waiter had brought my split and her Coke. "It's about Roger."

"Roger?" I asked. "Roger, my brother?"

"You know perfectly well that's the Roger I mean," she said. "I want you to level with me, Warren. I want to know why he hates me."

"I'm sure Roger doesn't hate you, Laurel," I said. "I don't know where you got that idea."

"He never comes to the phone when I call," she said. "And I know he can't be spending all his time at the library."

"He's awfully busy these days, I think."

"Roger looks straight through me at school," she said with a sigh. "He treats me as though I didn't exist." There was the beginning of a tear in her right eye. I tried to concentrate on my banana split.

"I don't see why you're wasting your time on Roger," I said. "He's a jerk." For a moment I hated Roger for making Laurel sad.

"I think he's wonderful," she said.

"You can do a lot better than Roger," I said. "Anytime."

"So he doesn't like me," she said. "I don't know why it took me so long to figure it out."

Although I am a firm believer in the right of the individual to keep a secret, this was one of those rare occasions when honesty was the best policy. Unless Laurel found out the truth about Roger's feelings toward her, she might keep mooning over him for the rest of her life.

"You're right," I said at last. "I don't think Roger likes you." I saw Laurel's lower lip tremble a little and I wondered if I really was doing the right thing. "But you've got to understand, Laurel—it isn't you. It's Roger. He's afraid you're better than he is."

"You're saying that to be nice, Warren," she said. "But don't think I don't appreciate it."

"I'm not," I said. "I'm saying it because Roger can be a jerk sometimes and you're nice. You're too nice for him."

Laurel took the napkin from the table and dabbed at her eyes with it. "There's one other thing, Warren," she said. "I don't want anyone else in town to know about our conversation today. I'd just die of embarrassment if anyone but you knew my secret."

"Don't worry," I said. "I won't tell anyone."

"But it's really important that you keep this secret."

"Trust me, Laurel," I said. "You don't know how good I am at keeping secrets."

That was in the winter, just after the first big snow storm, but I can tell that Laurel is still carrying the torch for Roger. Sometimes when I run into her after one of the high school basketball games or see her in the street she asks me how Roger is doing and I can tell she isn't over him yet. But she always asks me how I'm doing, too, so I know she isn't interested in me only because I'm Roger's brother. She likes me because I never breathed a word about her feeling for Roger to anyone.

And that's why I decided to tell Laurel O'Connor my own horrible secret. If she could trust me, I knew I could do the same for her. Besides, she was the only person in New Eden who might even be able to help me.

CHAPTER THREE

My Last Best Hope

Laurel's house is set back from the road by about fifty feet. At the beginning of April the green lawn in front was covered with patches of daffodils. As I rode my bike up the O'Connors' driveway, I could hear Laurel before I saw her. She was shooting baskets and dribbling with the precision of a Swiss watch. Trying not to disturb her, I got off my bike quietly and watched the steady *boom, swoosh, pat, pat, pat* as she threw one perfect basket after another into the hoop that hangs over the garage doors.

After she had scored another thirty points, Laurel caught the ball when it fell through the net. "Hi, Warren," she said. "What's up?"

"How come you're not sweating?" I asked. "You're not even breathing hard."

"It's called keeping in shape, Warren," she

said, pushing her long, blond hair behind her ears. "If you exercise all the time, you don't strain when you're playing. So you don't sweat."

"Never?" I asked. "Even Roger sweats."

"I sweat when I'm in competition," she said. "Maybe that's why Roger doesn't like me. He hates girls who sweat."

"I thought you were getting over that, Laurel," I said.

"I'm working at it," she said, a little sadly.

"You know, Laurel, I've never said a word to anyone about you and Roger, if you know what I mean."

"I'll always be grateful to you, Warren," she said. "You're a real friend to me, you know."

"I was thinking that you're not the only person in New Eden with a secret."

Laurel, I could see, was intrigued. "That sounds pretty mysterious," she said. "Could that person with a secret be someone we both know?"

"It's me, Laurel," I said. "I'm the one with a secret."

"You're too young to have secrets, Warren," she said.

"I'm not," I said. "I'm eleven and I've had this secret since I was eight. Maybe earlier, but I didn't know it was a secret then."

"People don't have real secrets until they're at least twelve," Laurel said.

"I'm ahead of my time," I said.

"Well, I'm sure it can't be a very bad secret, anyway, Warren."

"You're wrong, Laurel," I said. "It's a horrible secret. Really."

"Gosh, Warren," she said, looking concerned. "It sounds serious."

"It is, Laurel," I said. "Very."

"Do you want to go back to the patio and talk about it?" she asked.

"If it's okay with you," I said.

Laurel dropped the basketball and let it roll into a corner of the garage. Then we started to walk to the back of the house. The O'Connors have a big backyard with an apple orchard. Even in early spring, before all the leaves grow back on the trees, you can't see a single neighbor.

"Do you want a Coke?" she asked. "We're all out of banana splits."

"No thanks," I said. "I just want to talk."

"Okay," she said. "Let's sit down." By now Laurel was looking really serious, as though my horrible secret might be that I had some terminal disease or something. "Is it about a girl?" she asked slowly. "You can tell me, Warren."

"Laurel, please," I said, feeling genuinely

shocked. "I *am* eleven years old. I won't be having secrets about girls for at least two more years."

"Well, you did say you were ahead of your time."

"Yeah, but I'm not precocious," I said. "My secret is much more serious than girls. The fact is, I don't know how to throw a ball."

I waited a second or two for the shock to sink in.

"I can't catch a ball, either, if you want to know the whole truth," I added.

"You're only eleven, Warren," Laurel said. "Lots of kids can't catch or throw very well at your age. It takes time."

"Laurel," I said, trying to explain. "It's not that I can't throw or catch very well. My secret is that I can't do it at all. That's my horrible secret. Maybe it's hard for you to understand because you're so good at all that stuff."

"I understand, Warren," she said. "I really do."

"No, you don't," I said. "You see, I haven't told you all of it yet."

"Then tell me the whole story," she said. "I'm sitting down."

"Well, you see," I said, but the words were coming slowly. Maybe I didn't want to hear them myself. "You see, my secret is that I'm afraid of the ball. I get dizzy whenever someone throws one to me and I get paralyzed when I have to throw one back."

"This is pretty awful for you, isn't it?" she asked.

"It's terrible, Laurel. And you're the only person in the whole world that I can trust with the secret."

"How come no one else has figured it out yet?" she asked. "How come it's still a secret?"

"At school it's no problem because we just do push-ups or sit-ups and climb ropes and things in Mr. Simkins's gym class. After school you don't have to play anything if you don't want to. I tell the other guys that I have to do my homework or I'm helping my mom out at The Worm."

"Then why the panic now?" Laurel asked.

"It's Camp Hit-a-Homer," I explained. "It's the baseball camp Roger went to, the place where he ended up with the award for best camper. Well, Roger's convinced Dad that it's the best thing that ever happened to him. Dad says it wouldn't be fair if I didn't go, too. He doesn't want to deprive me of any of the advantages that Roger's had."

"But you could learn to play baseball at Camp Hit-a-Homer," Laurel said.

"Oh, no, Laurel," I said. "I'd die before I even got there. All the kids who go to Camp Hit-a-Homer are already good at baseball. They go because they want to get even better. If they saw me play, they'd laugh their heads off. They'd make fun of me. They'd call me a sissy. You're the only person I can trust, Laurel. And you know how to throw and catch a ball, too. That's why I came over to see you. I was sort of hoping you'd teach me. Give me private lessons, I mean."

"We're pals, aren't we?" Laurel asked. "Of course I'll give you lessons. What I don't understand is why you don't get Roger to help you out."

"Roger?" I asked. "Roger Fingler?"

"Yeah," Laurel said. "That's the one. Your brother."

"Roger can't solve my problem," I said. "He *is* the problem. If he ever found out, he'd never let me hear the end of it."

"How can you be so sure?"

"When your older brother is Roger Fingler, the superjock, it's tough being Warren Fingler, the super nonjock. He already thinks I'm a creep, Laurel. If he found out about this, I don't know *what* he'd think."

"So when do we start?" Laurel asked.

A terrible tremor went up and down my spine. Just the thought of trying scared me.

"You've got to start sometime," Laurel said. "And there's no time like the present, you know."

Laurel rose from her deck chair. Beside an apple tree lay a bat and softball. Laurel picked up the ball.

"Don't worry," she said. "No one can see. My brother's away at boarding school and Mom and Dad won't be home until it gets dark. Here," she said without any warning. "Catch."

Although we were only three feet away from one another, I put my hands in front of my face to defend myself from the oncoming ball. It tapped my shoulder gently and fell to the ground.

"I see what you mean," she said. "Look. You're never going to be able to catch it if you're going to be afraid. Don't worry. It's not going to bite you."

Laurel was smiling now, encouraging me. I wasn't afraid of her, I thought. Why should I be afraid of the ball?

"Now, pick up the ball," she said.

I did as I was told. By now Laurel had walked almost ten feet away from me. With some luck I might even be able to toss it that far.

"You're holding it wrong," she said.

"What do you mean?" I asked. "I'm just holding it."

"It's a ball, Warren," she said. "It's not a poisonous snake."

I tried to hold the ball a little more firmly. I

held my arm out in front of me and tossed the ball. Laurel raced in seven feet to make the catch.

"It's a start, Warren," she said. "Let's try again. I'll toss it to you this time and you try to catch it with both hands."

"Where do I keep them?" I asked.

"Keep what?" she asked.

"My hands," I said. "Where do they go?"

"They go at your side until you see where the ball is going."

"Okay," I said. "I think I can do that."

"And, Warren, it'll be a lot easier for you if you unclench your fists. Just try and relax a little."

I tried to let my arms swing freely as I waited for Laurel to throw the ball my way. This time it came at me even more slowly than it had before. Instinctively my hands tightened up as I reached for the ball. It hit my knuckles and fell to the ground.

"See, Warren," she said. "You're improving already."

"What are you talking about, Laurel?" I asked. "I missed the ball. Couldn't you see that?"

"I know, I know," she said patiently. "But you were awfully close."

"A miss is as good as a mile," I said.

26

"Not on your life," she said. "If you'd just had your fingers unclenched, you'd have caught it."

"You mean it?"

"I wouldn't kid you, Warren. Do you want to try and throw the ball back to me?"

"Maybe tomorrow, Laurel," I said. "I think I want to end my first lesson on a positive note."

If Laurel said I was improving, maybe I was. To tell you the truth, though, I wasn't really sure.

CHAPTER FOUR

Two Strikes and You're Out

The next day I decided I wasn't giving myself a fair chance. Here I was wanting to learn how to throw a ball and there was Laurel all willing to teach me. If ever a kid was missing out on a major opportunity, it was me.

As soon as I got home from school, I called up Laurel. All I had to say was, "Can you give me another lesson today?" and all she said was, "Get yourself over here in five minutes."

Laurel was at the back of her house when I got there.

"Ready for the next installment of *Mission Impossible*?" I asked.

"I don't want to hear any of that negative thinking, Warren," she said. "You will learn to play if you try. Get it?"

"I will learn to play if I try," I repeated after her. "How does that sound?"

"Not bad," she said. "Not bad at all. Say it to yourself two thousand times a day and you'll be fine."

Laurel walked three feet ahead of me. "The secret is to keep your eyes on the ball, Warren," she said. "When you've had some practice, your hands will just naturally come up to catch it. Just don't think about it too much."

"I can't help it," I said. "I'm no good at not thinking."

"Do just what I tell you," she said. "Okay?"

Laurel picked up the ball that lay beside the apple tree and tossed it, underhand, in my direction. Just as I'd promised, I watched it easing its way to me. Then when it got within three feet of me, I couldn't watch any longer. I froze up, I closed my eyes, and heard the ball drop with a thud in front of me.

"Better luck next time," Laurel said. "Now pick it up and toss it to me."

I knelt down and reached for the ball. I threw it to Laurel the only way I knew how.

"Try not to keep your hands so close to your chest," Laurel said. "Maybe you should start with underhand."

"I thought that *was* underhand," I replied.

"*This* is underhand," Laurel said as she tossed the ball back to me. Again I froze, only this time

it was worse than ever. The ball dropped in fro
of me.

"I can't, Laurel," I said. "I just can't."

"You're not giving up on me so soon, are you
she asked.

"But it's hopeless," I said.

"Just throw it back to me once more."

I picked up the ball and threw it. As usual,
wasn't overhand or underhand. It was sort of i
betweenhand and as usual it fell two feet in fro
of me.

"This time I *am* giving up and no one—n
even you—can talk me out of it."

"That's not the Warren Fingler *I* know,
Laurel said. "You can't give up now."

"I'm not taking this kind of torture an
longer," I said. "I know what the problem is now
I should have known it all along."

"Tell me what it is and we'll work on it to
gether," Laurel said.

"It's impossible," I said. "I don't want you t
take this personally, Laurel, but the problem is
well, it's that I throw . . ."

"Yes, Warren?"

"The problem is, I throw like a girl," I blurte
out. And without another word I walked towar
my bike.

For the next week, I lived my life as usual

waking up to the sound of Roger blending his breakfast, getting up to the sound of Roger running to the shower, pouring my cornflakes for breakfast, going to school, eating lunch in the cafeteria, getting through the afternoons, having dinner, watching TV, and going to bed.

The afternoons were the worst time. A couple of times I went over to see Arthur and Mrs. Lomax, but it wasn't the same anymore. Mostly, I spent my time riding my bike around the neighborhood, turning corners whenever I heard the sound of a baseball game in progress. By the end of the week the sound of a ball hitting a bat and some kid screaming "I got it!" was enough to leave my stomach in knots.

For ten days I licked my wounds and wondered if there was anyplace in this world for a clutz like me. Then one afternoon, as I was riding my bike by the Guiness Stables, it hit me. Right away I knew I had the answer to all my problems. Horse racing was what I had been searching for all my life—or at least for the last week. There was no catching or throwing involved in it. In fact, all you had to do was sit there.

The one drawback was that it wasn't cheap. Horses need a place to sleep and that costs money and they also eat like horses and that's not cheap either. What makes it even more expensive is that their trainers need to have places to sleep and food to eat, too. It's no wonder they call it the sport of kings.

Though my family isn't exactly poor, we're not exactly rich. The one stumbling block would be to get my parents to spring for the riding lessons. Mom and Dad give me the same allowance that every other eleven-year-old in New Eden gets and I wasn't due for a raise until I hit twelve. Somehow I had the feeling that even if I gave up candy and the movies I would still need a parental subsidy to make my dream come true.

It was a little after five when I left my bike in the garage. Dad's car and Mom's car were already there, which was kind of surprising, since neither of them usually gets home until around six.

"Hi, Warren," Mom said as I let myself in through the front door. "Have a good day?"

"Oh, fine, Mom," I said. "How come you're home early?"

"Your father is taking me out to dinner," she said. "We're celebrating."

"What's happened?" I asked.

Just then Dad walked in. He was wearing the blue blazer that doesn't say YOU'RE IN GOOD HANDS WITH FINGLER REAL ESTATE on it.

"I just sold the Victorian on River Road," he

said. "It's the one that's been on the market for three years."

"Gee, Dad," I said, "congratulations. Who's the lucky family?"

"Their name is McRae," he said. "They're moving here from Philadelphia."

If I hadn't wanted to keep Dad in a good mood, I would have explained to him that I meant the people who were moving *out* of New Eden.

"Do Roger and I have to go out, too?" I asked. The only thing that united Roger and me was our not liking to eat out.

"You and Roger can warm up the casserole we had last weekend," Mom said. "I've left it out on the counter."

"Does the sale mean we're rich now, Dad?" I asked.

"It means we're getting there, Warren," he said.

"Dad, I was wondering if maybe it would be okay if I took riding lessons over at the Guiness Stables?"

"Since when did you get interested in riding, Warren?" Dad asked.

"I've sort of had it in the back of my head for a while," I said. "The lessons are kind of expensive, but I thought we could use the Camp Hit-a-Homer money for them."

"I think you ought to try it," Dad said. "Roger seems to have a hold on all the team sports. It'd be good for you to try something different."

"Then I can take the lessons?"

"You bet."

"And I can forget about Camp Hit-a-Homer?"

"You can still go, Warren," Dad said. "We're almost rich, aren't we?"

A lump formed in my throat. Things were not working out as I had planned. "I don't think it's right for a kid to get riding lessons and Camp Hit-a-Homer all in the same year. It'll spoil my personality. I'll become a rotten brat. You'll hate me."

"You don't have to worry about that, Warren," Dad said. "Camp Hit-a-Homer might be good for your character."

That was the last thing Camp Hit-a-Homer would be good for, but I didn't know exactly how to tell Dad that. "I don't think I want to go to baseball camp all that much," was all I could say.

"I'll bet you feel different when July rolls along," Dad said.

"But I'll never be as good at baseball as Roger, even if I spend the rest of my life there."

Dad put his arm around my shoulder. "I don't care how well you play baseball," he said. "You know that, don't you?"

34

I nodded my head a little. "So why should I go to Camp Hit-a-Homer?" I asked.

"I think it would be good for you to spend a couple of weeks away from home," he said. "You could make new friends. I think it would help build up your confidence in yourself."

"My confidence doesn't need building up," I protested. "I'm so confident about myself, it's disgusting."

"I'm glad to hear that," Dad said, but I wasn't too sure that he believed me. "I'm glad about the riding lessons. Maybe you'll end up looking like another Matthew Bumkis."

"Just don't lose your head, dear," Mom said as she came back into the living room.

She and Dad went out the front door and I went to the kitchen to put the casserole in the oven. I decided not to think about Camp Hit-a-Homer, only about the riding lessons. I was in such a good mood that I even thought of putting Roger's portion in the blender. Tonight I was so happy that I didn't even mind if Roger was happy, too.

CHAPTER FIVE

The Sport of Kings

As anyone could have predicted, the next day turned out to be one of those monumental experiences that can change the course of a kid's life forever. In the morning Dad called Mr. Guiness from his office and arranged for my first lesson, and as soon as school let out, I rode my bike over to the stables.

Even though the barn door was open, I decided to knock.

"Mr. Guiness," I called. "It's me. Warren Fingler."

"In here," said a voice. "Come on in, son."

It was so dark inside that I couldn't see anything. The smell, however, was something else again. If you ever take up riding, you'll know what I mean.

"So you're the Fingler boy who wants to learn how to ride," said the voice. Through the darkness of the barn, I was unable to make out where the voice was coming from until it was about ten feet from where I was standing. "If you're serious about this riding stuff," the voice said, "you're going to have to get yourself a set of decent boots, you know."

"My father says he'll get me some this weekend," I said. "Are you Mr. Guiness?"

"That I am," he said. The man came closer. Even though I had lived in New Eden all my life, I was sure that I had never seen Mr. Guiness before. If I had, I would have remembered him because he was the tallest man I'd ever seen and his face was all brown and leathery and his hair was almost all white.

"I've never been on a horse before," I said. I didn't think it was necessary to let him know that I had never been *near* a horse before.

"A good thing, too, as far as I'm concerned," he said. "I won't have to unlearn you all the things I've had to unlearn a lot of other kids."

"What am I supposed to do first?" I asked.

"Get to know your horse," he said, leading me to the doors at the other end of the barn. After the darkness inside, the sunlight blinded me for a second and I was unable to see the corral directly in front of me. It wasn't very big, and besides, there was only one horse in it.

"That's your horse," Mr. Guiness said. "Her name's Spitfire."

I took a second look. If ever a horse didn't deserve a name like Spitfire, it was the animal that stood in the corral, munching the grass on the ground in front of her. You didn't need to know much about horses to know that Spitfire would be seeing the inside of a glue factory before long. I would be riding on the gentlest, most elderly horse that ever trod this earth.

"How old is she?" I asked Mr. Guiness.

"About thirteen," he said. "She and I have taught lots of boys and girls how to ride."

"Am I supposed to get on her right away?" I asked. Considering Spitfire's advanced years, I had a feeling there was no time to waste.

"She's all saddled up for you," said Mr. Guiness.

"What do I do first?"

"Today you're just going to get used to sitting on her," he said. "I'll lead you around the corral a few times so you can get the hang of it."

"No galloping?" I asked.

"You're not even going to trot until the third lesson," Mr. Guiness said.

"Sounds good to me," I said.

Mr. Guiness unlatched the gate and we both walked into the corral. Spitfire walked over to us without even being called.

"This is Warren," Mr. Guiness said to Spitfire, giving her a cube of sugar. "He's our new student."

"Hi, Spitfire," I said. "Mr. Guiness, where do I get on?"

"Fetch me that stool, boy, and I'll show you."

At one side of the corral was a stool, which I got and brought back to where Mr. Guiness was giving Spitfire another sugar cube. "Put it down and stand on it, boy," he said.

Nothing could have been simpler. I even patted Spitfire's neck. Spitfire didn't seem to mind.

"Now put your left foot in the stirrup, grab a hold of the saddle, and lift your right leg to the other side."

Throwing a ball should be so easy, I thought. I even liked the smell of the saddle. It looked as though Mr. Guiness polished it shiny smooth every night.

Mr. Guiness held on to the reins while I raised my right leg over Spitfire's back. The horse jerked a little, but it didn't startle me a bit. I knew I was safe in Mr. Guiness's hands.

My right leg went over the saddle easily enough and began its descent down Spitfire's side. My foot reached for the stirrup.

"How's it feel, boy?" Mr. Guiness asked.

"Pretty good," I said. "What do I do with my hands?"

"Just rest them on the saddle," Mr. Guiness said. "Right there." He pointed to a hump in front of me.

"And then what do I do with them?"

"You just leave them there, boy."

That was more like it, I thought, as Mr. Guiness gathered the reins in his right hand and began to lead Spitfire and me around the corral.

"Just get used to the feeling of being on a horse," he said. "That's the important thing right now. There'll be plenty of time for the fancy stuff later on."

"You mean galloping and jumping over fences?"

"That's about the size of it," he said.

By the time Mr. Guiness had led us around the corral twice, I was beginning to like riding a lot. I liked the idea of a sport where all you had to do was sit down, and most of all I liked the idea of a sport where you didn't have to worry about where to put your hands. In less than fifteen minutes I was feeling more confident than I had felt in a long, long time.

It was while I was humming the second chorus of "Back in the Saddle Again" that it happened. My right ankle began to itch and I reached down to scratch it.

As soon as I did, I accidentally pushed my foot into Spitfire's side. In less than an instant, she was off and away, tearing the reins from Mr. Guiness's hands.

"No, Spitfire, no," he shouted, but it was no use. The old horse was galloping around the corral at about a hundred miles an hour and I was clinging to her side, my left leg on the top of the saddle, my right leg under the horse. All that was holding me to her was my left hand, which clung to the mound of the saddle.

As Mr. Guiness ran behind us, I tried to pull myself back up. It was no use. I just couldn't hold on. The last thing I remember was hitting the ground and rolling free of the horse's hooves. A sharp jab of pain filled my shoulder and before I knew it I was unconscious.

CHAPTER SIX

A Lucky Break

Mr. Guiness says that I regained consciousness about fifteen seconds after I hit the ground, but I don't remember anything until I was lying in the back of his station wagon. I still felt foggy, but I didn't notice any pain except when I tried to raise my right arm. If you ever break your arm, you won't have to ask anyone. You'll know. Otherwise, it was almost comfortable back there, since Mr. Guiness had put a pillow under my head and covered me with a blanket that smelled like the stables.

"Can you hear me, boy?" Mr. Guiness asked.

"Oh, sure, Mr. Guiness," I said, a little feebly. "Where are we going?" Although I couldn't see anything from where I was lying, it seemed to me that we were going awfully fast.

"To the hospital. Your mom is going to meet us there."

"I think my arm's broken," I said.

"It sure sounded like that to me and Spitfire," he said.

"You could hear it breaking?" I asked. Breaking an arm didn't seem like much, but hearing it break must be horrible. "I'm sorry, Mr. Guiness," I said. "I didn't mean to fall off Spitfire."

"It wasn't your fault, son," he said. "It just happened."

It was nice of Mr. Guiness to say that, but it didn't keep me from realizing that it had taken me less than five seconds to ruin everything. That's when the arm started to hurt.

Mr. Guiness slowed down and turned a sharp corner. I figured we were pulling into the parking lot of Memorial Hospital. This is where a lot of people might get nervous, I suppose, but as far as I was concerned, it kept me from thinking of my latest flop. Mr. Guiness brought the car to a gentle stop. Within seconds a man in a white suit opened the back of the station wagon and another man in a white suit helped him push me onto a stretcher.

"I think I can walk," I said.

"Not until the doc's had a chance to check you over," said one of the orderlies.

They rolled me toward the emergency room entrance. Once we were inside, I saw that there were five or six other patients ahead waiting. The orderlies didn't seem to notice and pushed me into one of the examination rooms. I guess you get a lot more attention in a hospital if you have someone phone ahead.

"I'll wait for you out here, son," Mr. Guiness said. "I've never lost a student yet, so don't worry."

"I won't," I said. "I promise."

It was the first time I had been to New Eden Memorial since Mom and I had gone there eleven years before for me to get born. And just as the orderlies were transferring me from the stretcher to the examination table, Mom came running in.

"Oh, Warren," she said, running up to the table where I was lying. "How are you? Has the doctor come in to see you yet?"

"I'm Dr. Bradley, Mrs. Fingler," said a short, dark man I'd never seen before. "Warren, we're going to take some X rays of you and then we'll put you back together again. Mr. Guiness says you lost consciousness for a few seconds. How does the head feel?"

"Okay, I guess," I said. "I'm still a little dizzy."

Before I knew it, the orderlies were back to transfer me from the table to another stretcher. They rolled me to another room. They set me down on another table and left the room while a nurse X-rayed my arm and my head. In a few minutes the guys were back with the stretcher. Dr. Bradley was already looking at the photographs when I was wheeled back into the examining room.

"It looks like you broke your arm in three places," the doctor was saying, as though he were impressed with my achievement.

"Ouch," I said. "How are my chances?"

"For a complete recovery?" Dr. Bradley asked.

"No," I said, "just for survival."

"I'd say excellent. In fact, if you're worried about any permanent damage to your throwing arm, don't be. I'd say you'll be able to toss a ball as well as ever."

"I was afraid of that," I said, not caring if the doctor heard me or not. "How long will it take to heal?"

"A while, I'm afraid," he said. "We're going to put a cast on your arm this afternoon. You may be in it for several weeks. And you'll have to take it easy for a while after that. I'm sorry," Dr. Bradley said slowly. "I just don't want you to get your hopes up."

"I get the picture, doc," I said.

"And I can see you're going to be a very brave boy about it," Dr. Bradley said. "I bet you're not even going to cry, are you?"

The thought of the rest of the spring and most

of the summer without having to throw a ball filled me with such incredible joy that the pain in my right arm was totally unnoticeable. The orderlies switched me to yet another stretcher to take me to the plastering room.

The doctor started to wrap rolls of hot, milky-wet cloth around my arm, from my shoulder to my hand. Mom came in, still looking very worried. I let her hold my other hand. It seemed to make her feel better.

"Warren has a slight bruise on the right side of his head," Dr. Bradley said as he kept on rolling out the stuff for the cast and dipping it into the hot water. "It'll be tender for a few days. Except for the arm, that's all the damage he seems to have sustained."

"Thank heavens," Mom said.

"Am I going to spend the night here, Dr. Bradley?" I asked.

"That won't be necessary, Warren," he said. "You should be able to go home in about twenty minutes."

"In an ambulance?" I asked. "With the siren going?"

"I think you'll be okay in your mother's car," Dr. Bradley said.

I tried to hide my disappointment. Under the circumstances a noisy arrival at our house seemed only right. After all, I was seriously injured. It was a miracle that I had come through. You just had to take a look at Mom's face to know that.

The only consolation for not going home in an ambulance was the fact that the orderlies came back one more time to take me from the plastering room to Mom's car. On the way we ran into Mr. Guiness, who had been waiting in the emergency room all that time.

"How are you doing, son?" he asked as I was being wheeled through.

"Oh, Mr. Guiness," Mom said. "It was so nice of you to wait. Warren's going to be just fine."

"Give my regards to Spitfire," I said. "Tell her I'll be back for another lesson just as soon as I've recovered."

"That's what they say, boy," Mr. Guiness said. "Once you fall off a horse, you've got to get back on right away or you'll be afraid for the rest of your life. Get well, son," he said as he held the door for Mom, the orderly, and me. "Let me know if there's anything I can do."

When I tell you that there was no way I could thank Mr. Guiness enough for what had happened already, I mean it. As I saw it, falling off Spitfire was going to prove the best break I'd ever had.

CHAPTER SEVEN

Hail, the Conquering Hero (I)

Although I was disappointed to miss a ride in an ambulance, things started picking up as soon as I got home. The first thing was that Mom said I could take Thursday and Friday off from school to let my poor bones set a little. The other thing was that Mom decided to take the rest of the week off too so that she could take care of me. She would be there to make my meals and keep me comfortable and entertained all the time. If anything went wrong at The Worm, she would take care of it on the phone or go over in the afternoon when Roger would be home to take up his tour of duty.

Ordinarily, missing two afternoons of practice does not put Roger in a very friendly frame of mind. But somehow my injury had elevated my status in Roger's eyes and I was now being treated with something like respect. Right after Mom and I had explained everything to him, he started calling me "Champ." It was a big improvement over "Chump." Roger was actually turning into a nice person.

Roger led me from the car into the house as though I were some celebrity who had never visited the Fingler residence on Elm Street in New Eden before.

"Do you want to go up to your room to rest, Champ?" he asked.

"That's probably a good idea, Roger," Mom said. "Warren's probably exhausted. Does the arm still hurt, dear?"

"It's not too bad," I said bravely, even though the arm didn't hurt at all. The cast, however, was another matter. It felt like it weighed fifty pounds. "I'm not really tired. Maybe I'll just settle down in the den."

"Let me get you comfortable, Warren," Roger said.

"And I'll get you something to eat," Mom said.

"Well, maybe I could eat something," I said. "Maybe I could have some ice cream. It's supposed to be good for the bones, I think. And maybe some blueberry pie with it."

"I don't want you to spoil your appetite, dear," Mom said.

"Gee, Mom," I said, "let's just cross that bridge when we come to it."

It didn't come as any surprise that Mom would be the world's best nurse. When I had the chicken pox and the measles, she plied me with fruit juice and ice cream and magazines. The big surprise was Roger. As he showed me into the den, he plumped up the pillows on the couch and brought the coffee table up so I could put my feet up on it. As soon as I sat down, Roger put a pillow behind my back and another under my arm.

"Do you want me to turn on the TV?" he asked as he took the blanket from Dad's wing chair and rested it over my legs. Even though it was warm enough in the house, I thought it would be rude to tell Roger that I didn't need it. The poor guy was trying so hard and I didn't want to discourage him at the beginning.

"Maybe later," I said. "I'll let you know when."

"Do you want to talk about it?" he asked. "How fast were you going when the horse threw you?"

"Spitfire was going about a hundred miles an hour," I said. "Maybe a little less."

"Spitfire?" Roger exclaimed. "Spitfire must be one mean animal. You took the fall like a real hero," Roger said. "Mom said you didn't cry at all. Gosh, I don't even have the guts to get on a horse in the first place."

"You're kidding," I said.

"Honest," he said. "Horses scare the living daylights out of me. I'm real proud of you, Champ."

Maybe if Dad hadn't come home then, I would have explained to Roger that there was something that scared me, too. On the other hand, I might not have. Getting all this attention from Roger made me feel good and I didn't want to do anything to ruin it.

"Warren's a hero, Dad," Roger said as Mom and Dad came into the den.

"So I gathered," Dad said. "How are you feeling?"

"Not too bad," I said. "The doctor says it's going to take a long time to heal and Mom says I don't have to go back to school until Monday."

Dad handed me a box of peanut brittle and I opened it as soon as I got the words *Thank you* out of my mouth. A lot of people I know aren't too crazy about peanut brittle, but I love it. I took a slab of it from the box and offered the rest to Dad and Roger. Dad shook his head and Roger looked as though I had offered him poison. I stuffed a large chunk into my mouth and bit into it. In one momentous second I knew that I would never eat peanut brittle again, never even look at a box of the stuff again. Eating peanut brittle

sounds a lot like breaking three bones at once, if you want to know the truth. I closed the lid and put the box on the coffee table.

"I guess I'd better leave room for the ice cream and pie," I said.

Dad smiled and Roger looked relieved. He even asked me again if I wanted to look at TV. "And don't worry, Warren," he said, "if you want another channel, I'll be right here to change it for you."

I suppose I could have pointed out to Roger that I had broken my arm, not my leg, and was able to get off the couch and make it all ten feet to the set and turn the channel knob with my left hand. I might even be able to make it back to the couch. But having dedicated a large chunk of my childhood to changing the channels for Roger, I decided to let him do it himself.

For dinner Mom made my favorite, which is Swiss steak and mashed potatoes. For dessert there was another round of ice cream and pie, and I probably could have gotten away with seconds if I hadn't felt stuffed. Since I wasn't going to school the next day, Mom and Dad even allowed me to stay up late, a once-in-a-lifetime opportunity. I blew it by falling asleep in the middle of my favorite show. Dad and Roger had to carry me to bed.

Being an invalid really takes it out of you, I guess, because I slept until ten o'clock the next morning. I have Roger to thank for that since he didn't use the blender to make his breakfast. What woke me up, in fact, wasn't a noise but a smell. Waffles smothered in maple syrup and six strips of bacon, which Mom brought me on a tray.

After that I went back to sleep and didn't wake up until Mom decided I should get dressed and come down to lunch. I wasn't crazy about Mom helping me put on my clothes, but when your arm is encased in plaster, you don't get a choice. I could get my pants on, but the shirt was murder and tying shoelaces was impossible.

Anyway, it was while I was eating my three grilled cheese sandwiches and watching *Your Money or Your Life* that the flowers came. It was a big bouquet of something I don't know the name of and the card read GET WELL SOON, FROM MISS PRESLEY AND THE ENTIRE FIFTH GRADE.

About ten minutes later, while Mom was still trying to get the flowers into a vase, Mrs. Lomax stopped by with a chocolate cake. Just in the knick of time, too, because Mom hadn't had time to do anything special for dessert. After that it was pretty quiet until three o'clock, when Arthur himself made an appearance.

"How are you feeling?" he asked as he handed

me a new rock album, which was really nice considering Arthur hates all music written after 1750.

"Thanks, Arthur," I said. "The record's terrific and I'm feeling fine." How I was feeling was getting to be a little boring, but it's something we invalids have to be nice about, especially if people are going to give us presents.

Arthur didn't seem too interested in how I broke my arm, but I could tell that he was really getting off on what happened to me in the hospital. Maybe if Arthur doesn't turn out to be a concert pianist after all, he'll become a doctor instead.

Arthur stayed around talking for almost half an hour, which is a world's record as far as our conversations go, and then Miss Presley stopped by with some books and the homework assignments I'd miss. She said I should do them only if I was feeling up to it. She also told me that all the kids were planning a surprise for me when I got back to school.

To tell you the truth, by the end of the weekend I was getting a little bored being waited on. I'd had just about enough of daytime TV anyway.

CHAPTER EIGHT

Hail, the Conquering Hero (II)

Roger offered to help me on and off the school bus and carry my book bag, but Mom insisted on driving me to school on Monday. By the time we got there it was a quarter to nine and Miss Presley was already deep into long division. The first thing I saw was a huge, home-made sign that said WELCOME BACK WARREN. As soon as the kids saw me, they began to clap, and Miss Presley put down her pointer and came over to help me.

"We've all missed you, Warren," she said. "How are you feeling?"

"I'm feeling fine," I said for what seemed like the five hundredth time in four days. "And I want to thank each and every one of you for your cards and calls, and I want to thank you for the nice flowers, even if I'm not sure what kind of flowers they were." The class applauded, but not as hard as they had before. Arthur took my book bag to my desk.

As soon as I sat down, Miss Presley went back to the long division and the rest of the morning went on as usual. There was a social studies quiz, but Miss Presley said I didn't have to take it because I had missed the lessons.

"How can Warren take a test anyway?" Shirley Garfield said without raising her hand first. "Warren's right-handed. He's not going to be able to take a test ever again."

There was a loud groan from the rest of the class.

"Make him take the test with his left hand," said Claire Van Kemp. Claire has straight black hair and she wears round, black-rimmed glasses, too. She sits two rows behind me but I didn't have to look around to know who was talking. "It's not fair to the rest of us," Claire added.

"Oh, Miss Presley, you mustn't make him do that," Shirley said. "If you make right-handed people write with their left hands, it warps their personalities. Warren might grow up to be a mass murderer or something."

A hush fell on the room. Suddenly there was a cry from Arthur, who was sometimes a little late to understand things if they weren't set to music. "Warren's going to be a mass murderer?" he asked. "Warren Fingler?"

"That's what my mother says," Shirley said with an air of authority that is rare among people in my age group. Shirley is a little shorter than most of the kids in the fifth grade, but she more than makes up for it with all the blond curls that her mother piles on top of her head each morning. What makes Shirley stand out in the looks department is that she is the only girl in the whole school who carries a little purse with her at all times. When Shirley grows up, she's going to be a lady, I guess.

"Please, Shirley," Miss Presley said. "Warren is not a mass murderer and he's not going to become one, either."

"You'll have to talk to my mother about that," said Shirley. "My mother has very strong opinions on the subject."

"I don't care if he's a mass murderer or not," Claire Van Kemp said. "That's Warren's business. I just think he ought to take the test."

"Please, children," Miss Presley said. "Warren is going to take the test later in the week. Don't worry, Claire. And he's not going to take it with his left hand or his right hand, so you and your mother don't have to worry, Shirley."

"What's he going to do?" Randy Pratt asked. "Is he going to take it with his feet?" The whole class started to giggle and Randy laughed along at his own joke. Randy will do anything for a laugh. You get used to it after a while.

"He's going to take it orally," Miss Presley said.

"Like stomach medicine," Randy bellowed. This time he laughed before the rest of the class did.

"Not exactly," Miss Presley said. "I will quiz Warren verbally on the material and he'll tell me his answers rather than write them."

"How are you going to check for spelling?" Claire Van Kemp asked.

"I will see to it that the test is fair in every respect, Claire," Miss Presley said. She was beginning to lose patience with Claire, which was easy to understand. I'd lost patience with her by the time we were in second grade. "Now, Warren, why don't you catch up on some of your reading while I hand out the tests to the others?"

While they went to work on the test, I tried to read. But somehow my heart wasn't in the primary agricultural products of Minnesota. All I could think about was Claire Van Kemp and how much I hated her.

When I began to tell you all about New Eden, I should have warned you about Claire Van Kemp.

Claire Van Kemp is in a category all by herself. Maybe it would shed some light on the subject if I told you that the Van Kemp family has run New Eden for as long as anyone can remember. Claire's uncle owns the hardware store and her other uncle owns the two gas stations. On top of all that, her father has been first selectman for about twenty years.

Claire is following in her father's footsteps. When we were all in the third grade, it was Claire who decided we should elect a class president. I don't know what they do in other schools in other towns, but nobody in New Eden starts electing class officers until they're in high school.

"What's a president of the third grade going to do?" Shirley Garfield had asked Mr. Raben.

"Declare war on the second graders," Randy Pratt answered.

"My father says you're never too young to learn about how government works," Claire said.

"I don't want some other eight-year-old to tell me what to do," Randy said. "I've already got five older sisters for that." This time Randy wasn't trying to make a joke. Right then he sounded scared to death.

"I think the president of our class could lead certain class discussions," Mr. Raben said. "He or she could call on people who wanted to speak out on one thing or another."

"What do we have to talk about, anyway?" Arthur Lomax said after Mr. Raben had called on him. "It sounds like a waste of time to me." You can trust Arthur to get to the point.

"I think we should worry about these details after the election," Claire said, this time without raising her hand. "Right now I'd like to open the nominations," she said. "I nominate myself, Claire Van Kemp, for president." Claire's smile turned into a beam. It was as though she had given herself something for Christmas.

"You can't nominate yourself," Shirley Garfield said, as though she were shocked.

"You can vote for yourself," Claire said. "Why can't you nominate yourself, too?"

"It's not gracious," Shirley said.

"I don't care," Claire said. "I want to be president."

"Are there any other nominations?" Mr. Raben asked the class.

"I would like to nominate Patsy Conklin," Shirley said. "She would be a terrific president."

"Any seconds?" Mr. Raben asked.

Thirty voices saying "I second the nomination" rang through the air.

"How about Claire?" Greg Stockard asked.

"Doesn't someone have to second her nomination, too?"

"Yes, that's true," said Mr. Raben. "Do I hear a second for Claire Van Kemp?"

Silence.

"Shirley," Claire said, "don't forget who took you to the movies last Saturday."

"I second the nomination of Claire Van Kemp," said Shirley Garfield, "but I'm going to vote for Patsy Conklin."

The campaign didn't begin until the following week, when Claire set up a schedule of weekend barbecues where she force-fed every member of the third grade with hot dogs, hamburgers, and enough potato salad to make half the class sick to their stomachs. It didn't make anyone like Claire any better than they had before and Patsy Conklin won by a landslide. The trouble was that Patsy's parents moved to Chicago and took Patsy with them. Claire won by default.

At the end of the fourth grade we went through another election and Claire won unanimously. The reason was that no one had the nerve to run against her and she ended up being the only candidate. Since the class never got around to having any discussions, there wasn't any way for Claire to be a bad president of the class. On the other hand, you couldn't say Claire was good at being president, either. It's just that being head of things seemed to run in her family and Claire carried on the family tradition with an enthusiasm that made us want to throw up more than her potato salad had.

Just then the lunch bell rang and Miss Presley went around the room picking up the tests.

"How's Warren going to get his food?" Shirley asked Miss Presley. "He can't hold a tray in one hand, can he?"

It was something that neither Miss Presley nor I had thought about till then.

Miss Presley said, "I think we'll have to get a group of volunteers to get Warren's lunch for him until his arm is better."

"I would be very pleased to be a volunteer," Shirley said.

"I think I should be first," Arthur said. "He's my friend."

"I think I should be first," said Claire, "and then I think everyone else should have a chance in alphabetical order."

"Why should you be first?" Arthur asked. "Van Kemp is the second to last in alphabetical order."

"As long as I'm president of the class," Claire said, "it's my civic duty."

"That's a lovely gesture, Claire," said Miss Presley. "That's the way we should do it, I think."

"Thank you, Miss Presley," Claire said. "And may I take this opportunity to remind everyone that I would be very willing to run again for president of the sixth grade."

"Thank *you*, Claire," Miss Presley said. "But I don't think this is the time to start your campaign."

"Well, my offer still stands," Claire said. "Come on, Warren. I'll get you your lunch."

It was an offer I couldn't refuse.

CHAPTER NINE

Claire, the Good Samaritan

"What do you want me to get you?" Claire asked as she led me into the cafeteria.

"You mean there's a choice?" I asked. "There never used to be."

"Well, I could get you chocolate milk or regular," she said. "Hot dogs and beans are what you can't choose."

"I suppose I could have hot dogs or beans, couldn't I?" I asked. "That would be a choice."

From the look on Claire's face I could tell that this Good Samaritan business didn't come easily to her.

"Look, Warren," she said. "I don't really care if you only want a glass of water. It's no skin off my nose. Just tell me what you want and I'll get it for you."

"I want two hot dogs and some beans and some

chocolate milk and for dessert anything they have as long as it isn't Jell-O," I said, trying to do my part. "Do I have to stand in line?"

If there was anything I didn't need it was standing with Claire Van Kemp and letting her show me off to everyone else as one of her good deeds. There was another problem, too, but I didn't want to get into it. You see, at New Eden Middle School there are two lines in the cafeteria and the boys always use one of them and the girls use the other. Eating lunch at our school is a little like going to the bathroom, I guess. About twice a year, Mr. Pringle, the school principal, makes an announcement at assembly that it doesn't have to be that way, but no one ever listens to him. Even if they did, the girls would still sit at the girls' tables and the boys would still sit at the boys' tables.

I took a seat at the big table on the boys' side of the cafeteria while Claire went to get me my food. We had spent so much time debating the menu that Claire was the last person in line. By the time she got back and plopped my tray in front of me, Arthur and Randy and some of the other guys were almost through their food.

"Enjoy," Claire said. "It was a pleasure getting it for you. I just hope there's still some left in the kitchen for me."

"Thanks, Claire," I said. "I really appreciate it." I was sort of glad that Claire was already too far away to hear me.

"Tell us how you got thrown from the horse," Greg Stockard said. Greg is the captain of the fifth grade Little League team, which makes him the most popular kid in our class for reasons you should understand by now. "Was the horse's name really Spitfire?" he asked. "Were you really going sixty miles an hour?"

"Well," I said modestly, "the horse's name really was Spitfire, but she wasn't going that fast. I was!"

"Wow," Greg said, "how long are you going to be in that thing?"

"The doctor says a few weeks," I said.

"Wow," Greg said again. If he wanted me to tell the whole story, I was perfectly willing. The only problem was that Arthur looked positively bored, which I didn't blame him for since he'd already heard the story ten times. Randy Pratt didn't look too interested either. In fact, he was mostly interested in the hot dog that I hadn't got around to eating. When he's not making jokes, Randy spends most of his time on the lookout for free food.

Before I got around to deciding whether or not I was going to tell Greg the whole story, a hush came over the cafeteria. I turned around to see what was happening. There was Miss Presley wheeling in the largest cake I had ever seen— more than enough to feed the fourth, fifth, and sixth grades of New Eden Middle for a week. Maybe even their families, too.

All the kids in the lunchroom stood up right away and began singing "Welcome back, Warren" to what sounded like the tune of "Happy Birthday to You." By the time they finished the chorus Miss Presley and the cake were standing in front of me. I wished I had had a camera. On the cake, written in red and blue icing, were the words WELCOME BACK, WARREN and under it in green, black, and orange was someone sitting on a horse.

As I stood admiring the cake I felt a large hand fall across my shoulder. It was Mr. Simkins. Now ordinarily Mr. Simkins is the person I most dread in the whole town of New Eden. Mr. Simkins is the gym teacher for the middle school. Until this moment his only verbal communication with me consisted of "Come on, Fingler, keep those arms high" and "That wasn't a real push-up, Fingler. Don't let your belly touch the floor." My wheezy "Yes, sir" was usually drowned out by my struggle to keep breathing.

The only thing that makes Mr. Simkins even

remotely bearable is the rumor that he and Miss Presley are engaged to be engaged. I don't know what she sees in him, but I guess that's Miss Presley's horrible secret. Right now I wondered if he was going to have me make up for the knee bends I had missed the week before.

"It's my pleasure and privilege," he said, "to welcome Warren Fingler back to school." Up to that moment, I had had no idea that Mr. Simkins even knew my first name. "As I think most of you know by now, our own Warren Fingler suffered a grave injury last week when he was thrown from a horse, Spitfire by name, at Mr. Guiness's stables. Right now I want to salute Warren for his courage and his bravery and express our collective admiration for his initiative in taking up riding on his own."

For a moment I was afraid that Mr. Simkins was about to slap me on the back. Thanks to the weight of the cast, a slap could have knocked me over into the cake. Instead Mr. Simkins reached for one of the ball-point pens that was clipped to his shirt pocket.

"May I have the honor of being the first person to autograph your cast?" he asked.

I nodded my permission. He wrote, "To a great guy and a terrific sport, from Bart Simkins."

While Mr. Simkins tried to make the pen work on the cast, Miss Presley started to cut the cake and hand out pieces of it to everyone.

The kids gathered around to eat their cake and look at the autograph and Miss Presley let us stay ten minutes after the bell rang.

About half an hour before school let out, Miss Presley put aside the biology book and said, "I have an announcement to make, children."

"You're going to let us out early?" Marcie Lewis asked.

"There's more cake?" Randy Pratt asked.

"It's more exciting than either of those suggestions," Miss Presley said. "The Junior Chamber of Commerce has arranged a contest for all the students in the middle school to get Matthew Bumkis a new head. The student who, through his or her own initiative, raises the most money for the restoration of the statue in the village green wins a free trip to the state capital."

"Is that an overnight trip, Miss Presley?" Shirley Garfield asked.

"Yes, it is, Shirley."

"Are all expenses paid?" Shirley asked.

"Yes, Shirley. Everything is paid for. And the winner will get to have lunch with the governor."

"Will the winner's picture be in the paper and on TV?" Randy asked.

"I can't make you any promises about that," Miss Presley said, "but I wouldn't be at all surprised if it was."

"How can we raise money?" Randy Pratt asked. "We're too young to get jobs."

"That's where the initiative part comes in, Randy," Miss Presley said. "You have to think of some way to make money."

"How?" Randy asked.

"You could sell raffle tickets, for instance," she said. "Or you could sell cookies."

"Like the Girl Scouts?" Randy asked. "No thanks."

"Well, you might do something else," Miss Presley suggested. "Open a lemonade stand—that's an idea."

"But no one drinks lemonade except in July and August," Shirley said. "At least no one at my house does."

"Sell apple juice," Miss Presley said. "Sell Kool-Aid."

"Well, I suppose that would be okay," Shirley said.

"I think we should skip the whole contest," Claire Van Kemp said.

"I don't think I understand, Claire," Miss Presley said.

"Well, it seems to me that if anyone is going to have lunch with the governor, it ought to be me," Claire said. "After all, I am president of the class, aren't I?"

"That's not fair," Shirley said.

"*I* think it is," Claire said.

"Claire," Miss Presley said, "the Junior Chamber of Commerce says it's a contest. That's the arrangement."

"Okay," Claire said. "Let's get this show on the road. But everyone else should know they don't have a chance."

"Don't count on it, Claire," I said. "You never know."

In all the years I've known Claire Van Kemp I've never had a fight with her, mostly because she kind of scared me. But there was something in what she said and the way she said it that made me mad. Maybe it was all the attention I had been getting lately that gave me the confidence to speak up.

"Everyone knows I have more initiative than anyone else," she said. "There's no way I can lose."

"I bet I could raise more money than you could," I said.

"I doubt it, Warren," she said.

"I'll prove it," I said.

"Come on, Warren," she said. "I could beat you with one hand tied behind my back."

"And I'll beat you with one arm in a cast," I said.

Just then the bell rang, but for once in the history of the New Eden Middle School, no one started to get up. They were all too interested in what was going on between Claire and me.

"Is there anyone else in the class who would like to participate in the contest?" Miss Presley asked.

No one spoke.

"I guess that means it's between us, Claire," I said.

Claire gave me one of her mean smiles. I smiled right back at her. Somehow or other I was going to teach Claire a lesson she'd never forget.

CHAPTER TEN

Roger and His Muscle Milk

"How was school today, Champ?" Roger asked me. "Get through it okay?"

"Terrific," I said. "I'm going to raise more money than Claire Van Kemp so I can go to the state capital and have lunch with the governor."

"What's this all about?"

"It's for the Junior Chamber of Commerce," I said. "They're having some kind of initiative contest to see who can raise the most money to put Matthew Bumkis's head back on."

"I'm impressed," Roger said, pulling a handful of carrots from the fridge and placing them in the blender. Then he took a green pepper, a tomato, a stalk of celery, and shoved them in, too.

"Why don't you ask Mom to buy some V-Eight?" I asked as Roger started the machine.

"Wouldn't taste as fresh," he shouted over the noise. "Wouldn't have all the same nutrients."

The racket made it impossible to talk anymore. After a minute, Roger turned the machine off.

"Opening a can of V-Eight would be quieter," I said.

"You want some, Champ?" he asked. "It would make your bones heal faster."

To tell you the truth, I was touched by Roger's generosity. Nevertheless, I shook my head. Just looking at Roger's glop made my stomach feel weird.

"Hey, what's that on your cast?" he asked.

"It's an autograph," I said, barely paying attention. It was three hours after I had challenged Claire Van Kemp, but I was still as mad as could be. "Mr. Simkins made a big point of signing it today in front of everyone."

"Simkins autographed your cast?" Roger asked as he inspected the inscription. "I thought you said he hated you."

"We're regular buddies since I fell off the horse," I said.

"That's some kind of endorsement," Roger said. "Why don't you make the other kids pay to sign your cast?"

"You're kidding, aren't you?"

"Heck no," Roger said. "Kids always go for

76

that jock stuff. And you can use the money for the Jay Cees' contest."

"What contest?" Mom asked as she came in. "What's going on?"

"Warren's entering a contest to raise money for old Bumkis's head, Mom," he said. "I was telling him to make people pay to autograph his cast. If Jean-Claude Killy broke his leg, he could charge people to sign the cast, I bet."

"But, Roger, I'm not exactly a jock."

"If you fall off a horse, you're a jock," he said. "You even got Simkins's endorsement."

"What do you think, Mom?" I said.

"It depends on how much you want per autograph, I suppose, dear."

"Is fifty cents too much?" I asked.

"Make it a buck," Roger said.

"Even if Roger is right that anyone would sign it, you don't have room on it for more than twenty-five autographs," she said.

"See, Roger," I said. "That comes to only twenty-five bucks. I'm sure Claire can do better than that."

"I was only trying to help, Champ," Roger said.

"Miss Presley thinks we should sell things like cookies. What do you think?"

The idea of selling cookies didn't go down too

well with Mom. "Don't think I'm going to make cookies, Warren," she said. "I love you, but . . ."

"But, Mom," I said. "I don't know how to make cookies."

"And I don't even have the time to teach you how. You'll have to think of something else," she said. "The Jay Cees want to reward your initiative, not mine."

"This is really important, Mom," I said. "All the kids at school are counting on me to beat Claire for the trip to the state capital."

"Then let their mothers bake your cookies," she said. "You can put me down for two boxes."

Suddenly Roger let out a howl. "I got it, Warren," he yelled. "I've really got it."

"You know someone who'll make cookies for me to sell?" I asked.

"You're not going to make them yourself, Roger," Mom said, but it sounded more like a plea than a statement.

"It has nothing to do with cookies," Roger said excitedly. "And there's no way Warren can't go right to the top with it."

Now I was getting excited, too, waiting for Roger to let us in on his great idea.

"You can sell them glasses of my vegetable drink," he said. "They'll love it. We can open up a stand right in front of the house."

"Are you sure the kids'll buy it?" I asked.

"If you tell them that's all I ever drink, they'll be lined up for miles," Roger said. "I don't mean to brag, but you could even call it Roger Fingler's Muscle Milk. What do you think?"

"I think I'd better find out what the stuff tastes like first," I said.

There was about an inch of the glob left in the blender. I poured some into a glass and took a sip. It tasted just like it looked.

"I don't think it tastes that good, Roger," I said.

"It's not supposed to," he said. "No one but you would expect it to taste good."

"I don't get it," I said.

"It's supposed to make you strong and healthy," Roger said. "The kids will buy it because they want to be superjocks."

"Well, maybe we could add chocolate," I said. "You know, for the younger kids who haven't decided what they want to be yet."

"If that's what you want, kid, that's what you'll get," Roger said. "We'll have regular and chocolate muscle milk."

"What do you think, Mom?" I asked.

"If you and Roger make it yourselves, I'm for it, dear," she said. "Put me down for two glasses, but don't expect me to drink it."

"How much are we going to charge?" I asked.

"Fifty cents a glass, I think," Roger said. "A very small glass. You'll make a fortune."

"And you'll really help me make it?" I asked.

"You bet," he said.

"Gee, that's wonderful," I said. "I'm going to call Arthur right away. I want him to be the first to know."

I went into the den and dialed Arthur's number. With my good hand. It was Mrs. Lomax who answered.

"Hi, Mrs. Lomax," I said. "It's me. Warren Fingler."

"Hi, there, Warren," she said. "I hear you're going to have lunch with the governor. Congratulations."

"If I win the Jay Cees contest, I am," I said.

"How could you lose?" she said. "Do you want to speak with Arthur?"

"If he isn't practicing," I said.

I could hear Mrs. Lomax say, "Arthur, Warren wants to talk to you."

"Hi, Warren," he said when he came on the line. "Have you decided how you're going to beat Claire?"

"Nothing to it," I said. "This Saturday Roger and I are opening the first 'Roger Fingler Muscle Milk' concession in front of our house."

"Roger's doing it with you? Wow. What's muscle milk?" Arthur asked.

"It's the glop Roger drinks all the time," I said. "It's what keeps him in shape."

"Really? Does it help bodies grow in twelve ways?" Arthur asked.

"Do you have to ask?" I said. "You know what Roger looks like. Muscle milk should be good for at least twenty."

"What time does the stand open?"

"Around noon, I guess. This Saturday."

"Gee, Warren," Arthur said. "Why don't you wait another week?"

"Can't you make it?"

"Well, you see," he said, "I promised Claire that I'd go to her barbecue on Saturday. I can't go back on my word, can I?"

"Promised Claire?" I asked indignantly.

"She sort of made me promise, Warren. I'm sorry."

"How did she make you promise?"

"She wouldn't stop screaming at me until I did," he said. "I can't stand it when she screams."

"Did she make everyone else in school promise, too?" I asked.

"I think she must have screamed at everyone in town by now," Arthur said.

"Do you know what she's having at her cook-out?" I asked.

"She said hot dogs and hamburgers and fried chicken and potato salad," Arthur said.

"And you're going to pay for that sort of stuff?"

"Not the potato salad," he said. "I got sick the last time. Remember?"

"You'd better watch out for the rest of her stuff, too, unless you want to end up in the hospital the way I did."

"I don't think anyone's going to break an arm eating Claire's food, Warren."

"I meant having your stomach pumped, Arthur."

"Ugh," Arthur said.

"If I were you, I'd save my appetite and my money for muscle milk."

"Well, if you say so, Warren."

"And by the way, Arthur, it comes in regular and chocolate."

When I hung up the phone, I couldn't help smiling. It looked like Claire Van Kemp had finally met her match.

CHAPTER ELEVEN

Claire Gets Too Big for Her Britches

By the end of the week Claire had also gone into the memorial souvenir business. Installed on her desk at school was a basket filled with cardboard badges that anyone could have for a price. The badges were round and each one said HEADS UP FOR BUMKIS and each letter was drawn with a different color crayon. In addition to all her other talents, Claire was pretty fast with the scissors and crayons and the cardboard. She even had posters for her barbecue all over school. At least the "Welcome Back Warren" banner was still up.

"Shirley," Claire said as the fifth graders straggled into class on Friday morning, "I hope you will want to wear one of my buttons." Claire handed Shirley Garfield one of the badges. "I think this one would go very nicely with your coloring."

Shirley took the badge from Claire and held it

up to the light. "What do you mean, my coloring?" Shirley asked.

"Well," Claire said, "the yellow goes beautifully with your hair, I think, and the reds go just as well with your eyes."

"My eyes aren't red," Shirley cried. "They're hazel."

"But there are red highlights in them," Claire said. "Very becoming ones, I might add. Please wear the pin. I made it just for you. They're only fifty cents each. Maybe you'd like two."

"Well, you see, Claire," Shirley said, "I'm sort of short until I get my allowance tomorrow."

"Ah, just in time for my barbecue," Claire said. "You promised to come, Shirley. Remember?"

"Of course I do," Shirley said. "May I pay for the badge tomorrow?"

"Okay, I guess," Claire said, eyeing Shirley's purse. "Your credit's good with me." Claire opened a small black book on her desk and wrote SHIRLEY G. FIFTY CENTS.

Shirley pinned the badge on her blouse and sat down at her desk.

"Good morning, Claire," I said. "Do you have a badge for me, too? Something that goes with brown eyes and sandy hair?"

"I just might, Warren," she said. "Anything

for a good cause, you know. I was sorry you had to cancel your mulched milk stand, Warren."

"We postponed it till next weekend," I said, "in order to handle the crowds. And, anyway, it's Muscle Milk."

"What's mulched milk?" Randy Pratt asked.

"It's something Warren wants to sell to poor, innocent children," Claire said.

"Muscle Milk, Claire, *Roger Fingler's* Muscle Milk," I said. "And it's guaranteed to turn anyone into a jock."

"Roger Fingler? Wow. Will he be at the stand?" Randy asked. "But even if he is, I'm not letting something called mulched milk cross my lips."

"Ah," said Claire, "the voice of the people, Warren. I feel sorry for you."

"What do you mean, you feel sorry for me?" I asked.

"I hate to think of you wasting all that time making all your mulched milk. Excuse me, Muscle Milk."

"I won't be wasting my time," I said.

"She's saying you're not going to win, Warren," Randy said.

"I'm glad you see the light, Randy," Claire said. "Maybe you should clue in your friend here."

"Who says I'm not going to win?" I said. Claire was beginning to make me mad. "I *know* I'm going to win."

"It all has to do with diversification," she said. "You don't have it. You're a one-shot. It's hopeless."

"You think you're going to win because you have a basket of buttons and eight different kinds of greasy food?" I asked.

"Let's face it, Warren," Claire said. "The public likes a bit of grease now and then. You're coming, aren't you, Randy?"

"Wouldn't miss it for the world," Randy said. "You're sure you're going to have fried chicken?"

"Just for you, Randy," Claire said. "And don't forget the hot dogs and hamburgers."

"And the potato salad," I added. "No one will ever forget your potato salad, Claire. You should register it with the police as a lethal weapon."

"Do the authorities know about mulched milk?" Claire asked.

"I like Claire's potato salad," Randy said. "I had three helpings last year."

"And lived to tell about it, too," I said. "Good going, Randy."

"There's no reason why both of you can't have very successful events," Shirley Garfield said.

Randy, Claire, and I turned to her as she stood up at her desk and walked toward us. If there were two things that Shirley stood for, they were gracious living and keeping the peace. "Maybe it will all end up in a tie," she said.

"Impossible," Claire said. "Warren doesn't have my organization. He doesn't have my initiative."

"You don't need initiative to have a barbecue," I said. "Your father has one every other year when he runs for first selectman. It takes initiative to think up something like Muscle Milk."

"Hear, hear," Randy Pratt said. At last I had won him over to my side.

"Then you'll skip Claire's barbecue, Randy?" I asked.

"Are you kidding?" he asked. "I've been saving up for it."

"I thought you were on my side," I said.

"I am, Warren," he said. "But I like junk food, too."

"How dare you call my food junk?" Claire screamed.

"Children, children!" Miss Presley said. "Randy, Claire, Warren, Shirley, I want you all to sit down immediately. The bell has rung!"

The four of us looked around. All the other kids

were sitting at their desks and staring at us. Some of them were grinning. It was clear that our little conversation had not gone unnoticed.

Without another word, we all sat down at our desks. Miss Presley began to look a little calmer.

CHAPTER TWELVE

Fingler's Last Stand

The reports on Claire's barbecue were, I'm sorry to say, terrific. At five o'clock, Arthur stopped by on his way home to tell me all about it.

"First of all, it was even better than those cookouts Mr. Van Kemp has when he's running for office," Arthur said.

"I don't think I want to hear about it, Arthur," I said.

"You told me to tell you exactly what it was like," he said.

"That's true," I admitted. "Don't spare me any of the gory details. What was so special about it?"

"They had music for one thing," he said. "Live music. High school kids, too."

"Did you spend a lot of money?" I asked.

"You know I didn't," he said. "I'm saving up for Roger's Muscle Milk."

I looked at Arthur a little more closely for signs of ketchup smears. As far as I could tell, the kid was clean. I let him go home to practice for an hour before he had dinner.

About three seconds later the telephone rang. It was Shirley Garfield.

"It was lovely," Shirley said. "Mrs. Van Kemp had real tablecloths and stainless steel. There wasn't a piece of plastic in the whole place. I wish my mother had seen it."

When Randy Pratt called five minutes later, I wasn't sure how much more of this I could take.

"You wouldn't believe all the grub they had," Randy asked. "The hamburgers were *better* than McDonald's. Bigger, too."

"How was the chicken?" I asked in spite of myself.

"First rate," Randy said. "I must have spent a fortune, Warren. I just couldn't help myself."

"Did you save anything for Muscle Milk?" I asked.

"Not a dime," he said. "But don't worry. My mom is giving me an advance on my allowance."

"Well, that's the best news I've had all day, Randy," I said. "Do you know how much Claire made?"

"She was still counting the money when I left," he said. "It looked like quite a haul."

"I don't know how she pulled it off," I said.

"Well, you know the Van Kemps," Randy said. "When it comes to running for something or winning something, they all pitch in. Her father and her uncles were working at the barbecue, her mother ran the drink concession, and Claire . . ."

"Yeah," I said. "Tell me what Claire did."

"She did her part, Warren. She went around making change."

"Was there any food left?" I asked. "Or did you eat it all?"

"Oh, there was plenty left," he said.

"Which they had to throw out?"

"Not the Van Kemps," Randy said. "They just put it back in the freezer and wait for the next campaign. Have you got all your Muscle Milk ready?"

"Not yet," I said. "But don't worry. We're going to have enough to meet the demand. Enough to show Claire what initiative is all about."

The next day we went to work on the Muscle Milk. Roger even skipped *Wide World of Sports* to help. It's hard enough to grind celery and tomatoes and cucumbers with two hands. With one it's murder. By five o'clock Mom said we had to restore the kitchen to some kind of order so that she could make dinner for us.

"How much did you boys brew today?" she asked.

"It looks like almost three quarts," Roger said.

"That's impossible," I said. "We've been working all afternoon. We should have gallons."

"Take a look, Champ," Roger said.

I looked at the counter. To my horror, Roger was right. There were only three bottles of the glop.

"How am I going to beat Claire with only three quarts of the stuff?" I asked.

"Maybe you should charge ten dollars a glass," Mom said. She was trying to make a joke, but this time it wasn't funny.

"You know we can't," I said. "We can't charge more than fifty cents. What are we going to do?"

"You're going to have to work harder and faster," Mom said.

"Will you help?"

"I know it's an emergency, dear," she said. "Dad and I want to pay for the ingredients, but I've got too much going on at The Book Worm this week to help make anything. Maybe you can get someone else to help."

"Who?" I asked.

"Someone with another blender," she suggested.

That's when I thought of Laurel O'Connor. I knew that she would be willing to help and I was pretty sure that her mother had a blender, too. There was a hitch, though, and its name was Roger. Now that he was becoming a real pal, I didn't want to do anything to upset him.

"I know someone who could help us out," I said. "Someone with a blender."

"Call them up, Warren," Roger said. "What are you waiting for?"

"Well," I said, "the person I have in mind is Laurel."

"Laurel O'Connor?" he asked. "Since when did you get to know her?"

"Since I started fielding those telephone calls for you," I said. "She's really nice, Roger, and she's sort of one of my best friends now."

"Then get her on the phone," he said.

"But I thought you didn't like her so much," I said.

"If she can help us out, I'm all for it," he said.

I didn't waste a second calling up Laurel. She said she'd bring over not one but two blenders. That's my idea of a real friend.

Monday night when Laurel came over, we were able to make more than two gallons, Tuesday night we hit four, and by Thursday we had almost twenty. That was the night Laurel arrived with half a dozen posters under her arm.

"What do you think?" she asked as she spread them out on the dining room table.

Roger and I took a look. Right away I could tell that Roger was even more impressed than I was. In front of us were six large cardboard advertisements for ROGER FINGLER'S MUSCLE MILK—THE MILK OF CHAMPIONS.

"I thought we'd better do a little advertising," she said. "Hope you like them."

"They're really beautiful, Laurel," Roger said. "I didn't know you were so talented. That really does look like the muscle on my right arm, too."

Laurel smiled. "I tried my best, you know, for Warren's sake. I want him to win this contest as badly as you do."

"Who says we call it quits on the Muscle Milk after tonight?" Roger said.

"Do you think we have enough for Saturday?" I asked. "Enough to beat Claire Van Kemp, I mean?"

"We've got twenty gallons, don't we?" Roger asked. "We're going to win in nothing flat, Champ. Besides," he said, "I was thinking we could all do with a little rest."

"I'm for that," I said. "I've got a lot of television to catch up on."

"And I was wondering if maybe Laurel

wouldn't mind going to the movies with me tomorrow night," Roger said. "If she wants to, that is."

The way Roger was looking at Laurel made me think he thought she wasn't going to say yes. "Do you want to, Laurel?" he asked.

"I'd like to, Roger," she said. "That would be nice." And when Roger offered to walk Laurel home afterward, she gave me the biggest wink.

We opened for business on Saturday at ten o'clock. The way we decided to arrange it was for Roger to handle the regular Muscle Milk and Laurel to take care of the chocolate-flavored. I would sit between them and collect the money.

As anyone could have predicted, Randy Pratt was the first in line.

"Which do you want, Randy?" I asked as nicely as I could. "Regular or chocolate-flavored? Why not try both?"

"I want the regular," he said.

Randy handed me fifty cents.

"That's one regular for Randy Pratt," I said to Roger.

"Coming right up, boss," Roger said as he gave Randy one of the plastic cups.

"Thanks," Randy said. "I didn't know this stuff would be green. I've never drunk anything green."

Randy took a big gulp. A split second later, he looked as though he wished he hadn't.

"Maybe you'd prefer chocolate-flavored," I said. "It's on the house."

Laurel handed Randy a cup. Randy took a sip. This time he looked like he was going to be sick.

"This stuff is poison," he said, and then he repeated it to the other kids who were lining up behind him. "This stuff is poison. The green stuff is rotten and the chocolate stuff is poison."

"It's not poison," I said. "It's delicious. Maybe it's an acquired taste. Maybe it takes a little getting used to."

"No one ever gets used to poison," Randy shouted. "This stuff could kill!"

"It doesn't kill you," I said, only really I was shouting, too. "It makes you strong in lots of ways. Look at Roger. He drinks it three times a day."

"In that case," Randy said, "your brother's stomach must be made out of cast iron. I want my money back."

"Okay, okay," I said. "You can have your money back. Just stop shouting. You're scaring the other kids."

It was too late. All the other kids had heard Randy screaming and were moving slowly away from the stand. Some of them were beginning to warn the other kids who were coming down Elm Street.

"If I die," Randy said, "they're going to put you in jail and throw away the key."

"Well, maybe it's not to everyone's taste," I said, but I could see it wasn't going to make any difference. Already the kids were looking at me as though I had committed some terrible crime.

"Maybe Shirley Garfield's mother was right," Randy said as he began to run. "Maybe you are a mass murderer."

"That's not what she said," I shouted. "She said I might turn out to be a mass murderer when I grew up. I'm still only eleven!"

The situation was desperate, I knew that.

"Look," I said to the rest of the kids who were still hanging around, staring at Roger, Laurel, and me. "Just because one person happens not to like Muscle Milk all that much doesn't mean the rest of you won't love it. I'm so confident that Muscle Milk is great stuff that I'm going to give, that's right, give it away for the next ten minutes. After that you'll have to line up to buy the stuff."

None of the kids moved forward.

"Arthur," I said. "Come on. Take a taste and tell the kids what you think."

"Do I have to?" he asked.

"Yes," I said, "you have to."

Very slowly Arthur came up to the stand. Roger poured him a cup. Arthur took a sip.

"Well, what do you think?" I asked. I had a feeling that my future hung in the balance.

Arthur swallowed very carefully. "It's very . . . it's very . . ." he mumbled.

"Come on, Arthur," I said. "Just tell us what you think."

"It's very . . . terrible," he said. "I'm sorry, Warren. I really tried to like it. It's just awful."

Within seconds Arthur and the rest of the kids had scattered. All that remained were Laurel and Roger and twenty gallons of Muscle Milk.

"Let's keep the stand going," Laurel said. "Someone else is bound to come along and like Muscle Milk."

"No, they won't," I said. "In ten minutes Randy Pratt will have spread the word and no one will be caught dead within five blocks of this place."

"I guess it's all my fault," Roger said. "I didn't know, Champ. I've loused up everything for you, haven't I?"

The look on Roger's face made me feel worse than I ever had before. I've never seen anyone look sadder.

"No, you haven't," I said. "You did everything

right. You did everything you could to help me. It's not your fault no one else in town has any taste."

"Thanks, Champ," he said. "I wanted to be a good brother to you, to help you the way a brother should."

"Roger," I said, "I don't care about winning the Jay Cees' contest anyway. Let Claire Van Kemp win. You're the best brother that ever was."

"You're a pretty terrific brother, too, Warren," he said. "I've always thought so."

"You have?" I asked.

"You know something?" Laurel said. "I think you're both pretty terrific."

The funny thing is that I meant what I'd said to Roger. Ever since I'd broken my arm, he'd been really nice to me. He'd even been really nice to Laurel, too. If things kept up like this, I'd start feeling sorry that I had suggested a couple times that he might not be the brightest person in the world. As it was, I started to drink Muscle Milk every morning with Roger.

What I didn't mean was the part about losing the Jay Cees' contest to Claire. The truth is I minded a lot. I minded it when the Muscle Milk flopped and I minded it even more the next week at school when everyone started ribbing me about it. I was prepared to take jokes from Randy, from Claire, but when Shirley Garfield said that she was sorry "not to have attended the riot," it was too much. My local hero status was now zilch.

The worst part came at the end of the week when Miss Presley asked for a progress report on how Claire and I had been doing in our efforts to raise money for Matthew Bumkis's head.

"Well, Miss Presley," Claire said as she stood up, "so far I've raised a hundred eighty-four dollars and seventy-five cents. Make that a hundred eighty-five twenty-five if Shirley Garfield coughs up the fifty cents she owes me for the Bumkis badge."

"I will pay you at the beginning of the week, Claire," Shirley said, "without fail."

"And you, Warren?" Miss Presley asked. "How much have you collected?"

"Oh," I said, "not so much, I guess."

"I'm sorry, Warren," Miss Presley said. "I'm afraid I didn't hear you."

It was no use. "I've raised a dollar fifty, Miss Presley," I said. Somehow I didn't feel like mentioning that fifty cents of that was from Randy and the dollar was from my mother.

"You shouldn't be embarrassed," Miss Presley

said. "There are still ten days left. Maybe you can come up with some other way to raise money for the project. Do you have any more money raising to do, Claire?"

"No, Miss Presley," she said, only this time she didn't bother to stand up, "I think I've done everything there is to be done, don't you?"

"It's a very impressive accomplishment," said Miss Presley, "and you have good reason to be proud. Warren, do you have any other plans?"

"Well," I said. I don't know why I was standing up but I was. "I want to tell everyone how sorry I am that Muscle Milk wasn't as successful as I hoped it would be. It really is a very good drink and it's very good for you, too, only now no one will know because my mom made me and my brother dump it at the landfill site because she was afraid of what it might do to our plumbing." For the first time in my life I couldn't think of anything else to say. However, that didn't mean I was going to stop talking and sit down. And then, out of nowhere, it hit me. A brainstorm!

"I guess this is as good a time as any to announce my second fund-raising project," I said. "It's an exhibition baseball game and I want to invite everyone in this class to play in it. The best part is that my brother Roger and Laurel O'Connor are going to play, too."

"Laurel O'Connor?" I heard Shirley Garfield ask. "She's my hero."

"Well, Roger and Laurel are going to round up all the other big athletes in the high school and they're all going to play with us," I heard myself say. "Unfortunately, I won't be able to play with you on account of my arm, but I hope everyone here will play and that everyone else will come and watch, even though everyone has to pay seventy-five cents toward Matthew Bumkis's head."

"Gee," said Greg Stockard. "I'll get to play with Roger Fingler. That's incredible. I'll sure be there. When is it?"

"It's after school next Wednesday," I said. It seemed like as good a time as any.

"Where is it?" Randy Pratt asked.

"At the high school," I said. That part was easy. The high school diamond had bleachers.

"And you're not going to have any Muscle Milk?" Randy Pratt asked.

"No Muscle Milk," I said. "That's a promise."

Suddenly the class burst into applause and I felt reinstated into my local-hero, minor-celebrity status.

"Class, class," Miss Presley said, trying to bring things back to order. "Warren, are you finished now?"

"Yes, Miss Presley," I said.

"Then you may sit down."

I bowed a little to the class. As I took my seat, the bell rang, so I got up again.

Right away almost the whole class was circling me and asking all sorts of questions about Roger and Laurel and how I'd come up with the idea and was it hard to convince them to join in the game. Greg Stockard asked if he could autograph my cast. I said sure and all the other kids wanted to sign it, too. It looked to me like I was going to get a lot of credit for a baseball game that I wouldn't have to play in. It was like having your cake and eating it, too. The fact that I might have to pay the consequences for not having the baseball game organized before I got up to speak— for promising to have Roger and Laurel there without having asked them first—was buried somewhere in the back of my mind.

As soon as I got out of school, I saw Mom's car in the parking lot.

"Warren, you didn't forget, did you? Today's the day you have your checkup with Dr. Bradley."

As a matter of fact, I had forgotten. And about an hour later I wished I hadn't been born. When we got to the hospital, Dr. Bradley X-rayed my arm and then he congratulated me on my recovery. It was a miracle, he said. Never before had he seen an arm broken in three places heal so quickly.

With that, he pulled out a lethal-looking weapon that looked like a miniature buzz saw and started to take off the cast, autographs and all. When he had removed it all, he wrapped my arm in an Ace bandage and told me I should wear it for a few days.

I knew that people usually got what they deserved when they did something wrong, but I doubted anyone had ever got what they deserved so quickly. All the way home from the hospital, I kept wondering how I could have gotten myself into this fix.

"You don't seem all that pleased to be ship-shape again," Mom said.

"Oh, I'm happy," I lied. "I'm real happy. I just don't understand how it happened."

"Well, darling, maybe it *was* the Muscle Milk," she said.

I slumped even lower in my seat.

CHAPTER THIRTEEN

The Way the Ball Bounces

In all fairness to Dr. Bradley, I have to admit that he was only doing his job. And when he buzzed off the cast he cut in between the autographs so I could glue back the cast when I got home and keep it as a souvenir.

"Keep it in a plastic bag," he said. "Those things begin to smell after a while."

"Yes, sir," I said. "I'll keep that in mind." Maybe I'll put it over the mantel, I thought sourly.

Was it the Muscle Milk? I wondered. Or was I simply the victim of an overly healthy body? Mostly, however, I knew that I was the victim of an overly active imagination and an overly active mouth. How could I have stood up in front of a whole roomful of people and promised them something that I probably wouldn't be able to pull off? And how could I promise something that was bound to ruin me even if Roger and Laurel decided to go along with it? Without the cast, I would have to play. My days were numbered no matter which way things went. It was easy enough for me to understand why I had done it. What I couldn't understand was how. As Dad says, an explanation is not the same as an excuse.

When Mom and I drove into the driveway, there was Roger shooting baskets with Laurel O'Connor. I'm not sure what brought about the change in Roger's feelings for Laurel, but it hadn't escaped my notice that the two of them had been spending a lot of time together since the Muscle Milk fiasco. Twice they had gone to the library to study and once Roger had taken Laurel to the movies. It was the only good thing that had come out of the whole mess.

"Hey, Champ, you got rid of your cast," Roger said while he dribbled toward the garage door.

"Oh, yeah," I said. "Dr. Bradley says it's a miracle."

"You don't seem too happy about it, Champ," Roger said. "Why the long face?"

I waited until Mom had gone into the house before telling them.

"I've done something really dumb," I said. "I wouldn't blame either one of you for killing me."

"It can't be as bad as all that," Laurel said.

"It's worse," I said. "I got carried away in school today and promised the kids that you and Roger would get the high school jocks to play a baseball game with our class."

"And you're going to charge admission, huh?" she asked.

"Right," I said. "I thought I could make enough money to beat Claire Van Kemp. Tomorrow I'm going to school and tell everyone the truth. I'm ready to face the music."

"Not so fast," Roger said. "What if we could round up enough people for a game? It might be kind of fun for us, too."

"How many are there in your class, Warren?" Laurel asked.

"Twenty-seven, including me."

"And the point is that you want everyone to have a chance to play with a high schooler, right?"

"That's the idea," I said. "Of course, my arm's still weak so I won't be able to play, but everyone else is dying to."

"When's the game?" Roger asked.

"A week from Wednesday," I said. "As soon as school lets out."

"You'll be fine by then," Roger said.

"Don't count on it," I said. "These things are tricky."

"In ten days you'll be terrific," Roger said. "It wouldn't be the same if you didn't play, Warren. It's important to me."

I turned to Laurel. She was the only person in the world who knew what I was going through. But just like the last time, there was no way she could help me.

"Laurel," Roger said, "I think we've got some heavy telephoning to do tonight. You call the gals and I'll call the guys. We should have a high school celebrity team put together in no time flat."

It was probably the nicest thing Roger had ever done for me. And it was going to be the worst thing that probably ever happened to me, too.

During the next ten days I often wondered how much better things would be if I'd gone to school the next day and announced to one and all that the game was off. The kids would have hissed and booed. Miss Presley would have given me a lecture, and no one would have spoken to me again.

But since Roger and Laurel were the most popular people at New Eden High, every single person they asked wanted to play in the game. And then Mom and Dad started getting into the act. Dad took a hundred tickets to sell at his office and Mom took a hundred and fifty to sell at The Worm. Laurel and Roger sold another two hundred, and in spite of my worst efforts, I sold a ticket to every kid at the middle school.

The final straw was that the day of the game turned out to be the single most beautiful day anyone in New Eden could remember. There wasn't a cloud in the sky from the moment the sun came up. I ought to know because I didn't sleep a wink the night before and I saw the sunrise. Only a late spring snowfall or an early hurricane could save me now.

True to form, I had no such luck. In fact, the only good thing about that day is that it has become something of a blur. They say that years after a horrible ordeal you begin to forget all the things that really were so horrible. In my case, I began to forget everything as soon as it happened. If it had been possible, I would have forgotten even earlier.

Roger made me drink Muscle Milk for breakfast. I don't remember lunch at all, probably because I was too nervous to eat anything. The only thing I do remember is that Claire came up to me in the cafeteria and said she couldn't come to the baseball game because she had other plans. At least there was one person in New Eden who wouldn't be a witness.

When school let out at three, all the kids walked over to the high school. Now I knew what condemned prisoners felt like on their way to the electric chair. They were lucky, I thought. I had to live after the execution.

Roger was going to be captain of one team and Laurel was going to be captain of the other team. Three of the high schoolers were going to be on his team and the other four would be on Laurel's. In his own modest way Roger had decided that, since he was the best athlete in town, he was probably good enough for two.

The rest of the kids had to pick cards from a barrel to see what innings they would play and what position. And since Claire wasn't going to be there, one lucky kid would get to play six innings instead of three.

"It's me!" Greg Stockard shouted. "It's me! I get to play six innings!"

"I'm a shortstop on Laurel's team," Shirley Garfield said. "I'm in the fourth, fifth, and sixth innings. I'm so happy. What's a shortstop?"

Laurel stepped in to explain to Shirley what shortstop was while the other kids picked their

111

cards. When my turn came, I picked "Right Field, Roger's Team, Seventh, Eighth, and Ninth Innings."

That was when the real panic set in. I didn't know which field was right and which was left. I wished I had the nerve to ask someone.

Roger and Laurel wrapped their hands around a bat to see which team would be up first. Roger's team won and Laurel's team headed for the field. As I headed off the field, I looked to the stands. They were packed with everyone I knew, everyone I wanted to keep my secret from, everyone who would be talking about my disgrace until the day I died.

Roger says a little panic is good for your game. I'm not sure. Panic may sharpen other people's senses but it turns me into a zombie. Maybe that's why everything got even blurrier than before.

I remember that somewhere in the second inning Laurel hit a home run, and that somewhere in the fifth Greg Stockard got on base. I can't explain how the score got to be six to four our favor by the time the seventh inning rolled around.

"Third team," Roger shouted at the nine of us who had not played yet. "My team up at bat," he commanded. "Laurel's team to the field."

Well, at least I was going to be spared the indignity of not finding right field for a little while longer. And because Roger had put me at the end of the batting order I would be spared the misery of striking out for a little longer, too.

Even though Laurel pitched really slowly to the fifth graders, the first three batters struck out right away. As soon as the catcher had the last strike ball in his mitt, Laurel's team raced toward home plate and all the kids on Roger's team started to run to the field.

"Come on, Warren," Roger said. "You're supposed to run out there, not walk."

"Run where?" I asked.

"You're right field," he said. "You're supposed to remember that."

"By the way, Roger, could you tell me how I might go about finding right field?"

"You're kidding, aren't you?" he asked.

"Roger, I'm serious," I said. "I knew but I forgot."

"You've got a bad case of nerves, haven't you, Warren?" he asked.

"I guess I'm a little excited," I said. "That's all."

"It's not going to be the end of the world," he said. "No matter what happens."

"What are you talking about?" I asked.

"I know," he said. "I found out last night."

"Laurel?"

"Yes, she told me."

"She promised not to tell anyone," I said. "She promised."

"She was trying to help, Warren," he said. "You should have told me yourself."

"I didn't want you to be disappointed in me," I said.

"For such a bright kid, you can be pretty dumb," he said.

"Roger," I said, "try not to let anyone get on base. I'll never ask you for anything else as long as I live."

"I'll do what I can," he said.

Roger walked to the pitcher's mound. I held my breath. I was very mad at Laurel and then I decided I wasn't mad at her at all. I was glad she'd told Roger. I was glad he wasn't disappointed in me. Now all I had to worry about were all the other people who live in New Eden.

Roger retired Laurel's team without a hit. If he could only keep it up for two more innings, I'd be saved. If we could keep our two-run lead, it would be even better. It wasn't much, but it was enough to get me through my one turn at bat. I struck out, but so had lots of other kids.

114

Only they had been able to keep their eyes open when they were up.

But at the bottom of the ninth inning Roger let Shirley Garfield get a base hit and he walked Greg Stockard. As if that weren't bad enough, it was Laurel's turn at bat.

"Come on, Laurel," her team was yelling. "Hit it out of sight. Hit it out of sight."

Roger began to wind up for the pitch. Even if he was going with her, it didn't keep him from serving his fastest pitch.

The ball whizzed across the plate.

"Strike one," yelled Mr. Simkins, who was the umpire.

Roger wound up and pitched again.

"Strike two," Mr. Simkins shouted.

If Roger could only make her strike out, I'd be home safe, I thought. And if she's going to hit it, please let it be the biggest home run in the history of New Eden. Let the ball go so far that no one, absolutely no one, would be able to catch it. Please, God, I prayed. Let Laurel strike out or hit a homer.

Roger wound up and pitched. All eyes were on Laurel. She went for it. As her bat connected with the ball, there was the loudest noise I ever heard.

"It's all yours, Warren," Roger yelled at me. "Go for it!"

Then I saw it. It was soaring higher and higher into the sky. You would have thought that it might never come down again. But it did. It made a small arc in the air and began its descent.

"Go after it, Warren," Roger was yelling at me. "Keep your eye on it. Keep your eye on the ball."

Before the old fears could grab me, I started running backward. Even if I'd been running forward, I don't think I could have gone faster. As the ball began to fall toward me, the sun got in my eyes and I couldn't see anything at all.

Roger was yelling at me, "Not so far, Warren! Watch out!" but I was running too fast to stop.

I heard the ball hit the fence behind me a split second before I charged into it. A sharp jab of pain filled my left arm as I fell to the ground. It was like a replay of how I had felt when I had fallen from Spitfire.

The only difference was that in my right hand I held the ball. That was all I remember before I lost consciousness.

CHAPTER FOURTEEN

How It Ended

The rest of the story is a matter of public record. Claire won the Jay Cees' contest and I came in second. What I didn't know until after the game was that Claire's plans for the afternoon included selling all the left-overs from her barbecue from the back of a truck that her family had parked in front of the high school. Everyone who spent seventy-five cents to come to the game spent another seventy-five cents at the stand on their way home. When it comes to initiative, I guess that I have to hand it to Claire Van Kemp.

I didn't mind so much losing the contest. As soon as I regained consciousness, I could hear the ambulance siren in the distance. This time, at least, I was going to enter Memorial Hospital in style. Once I got there, Dr. Bradley said that my second break was as beautiful as the first. It made me proud.

Since then life has returned to normal, more or less. After a couple of days at home, I went back to school, but Miss Presley and the kids didn't give me another cake. I guess they figure one a year is enough. Even so, Mr. Simkins told me that what with breaking my right arm horseback riding and my left playing baseball I was getting to be an all-around athlete. Which made me feel pretty good, too.

Things are pretty good between Roger and me, too. I still wake up every morning to the sound of him blending his Muscle Milk, but nowadays I have some of it, too, along with cornflakes. On the nights when Roger isn't studying with Laurel or taking her out to the movies, he tells me some of the finer points of baseball he's going to teach me when my arm gets better.

Thanks to the arm, Camp Hit-a-Homer is definitely out for this summer. I guess I should be grateful, but I'm not sure I am. Maybe if Roger and Laurel are willing to go to all the effort of teaching me to throw and catch a ball, I might end up being pretty fair at it. Sometimes I think that next summer or maybe the summer after I might even be willing to go there.

I figure that if you can live through what I've lived through, you shouldn't be afraid of a little ball, no matter how fast it's coming at you.